The Tiara Club

at Diamond Turrets

For Hero, with love and thanks xxx
VF
With very special thanks to JD

www.tiaraclub.co.uk

ORCHARD BOOKS
338 Euston Road, London NW1 3BH
Orchard Books Australia
Level 17/207 Kent St, Sydney, NSW 2000

A Paperback Original
First published in Great Britain in 2009
Text copyright © Vivian French 2009
Cover illustration copyright © Sarah Gibb 2009
Inside illustrations copyright © Orchard Books 2009

The right of Vivian French to be identified as the author of this
work has been asserted by her in accordance with the Copyright,
Designs and Patents Act 1988.

A CIP catalogue record for this book is available
from the British Library.

ISBN 978 1 84616 876 5

1 3 5 7 9 10 8 6 4 2

Printed in Great Britain

Orchard Books is a division of Hachette Children's Books,
an Hachette UK company
www.hachette.co.uk

The Tiara Club
at Diamond Turrets

Princess Bethany
and the Lost Piglet

By Vivian French

ORCHARD BOOKS

The Royal Palace Academy
for the Preparation of Perfect Princesses

(Known to our students as "*The Princess Academy*")

OUR SCHOOL MOTTO:
A Perfect Princess always thinks of others
before herself, and is kind, caring and truthful.

Diamond Turrets offers a complete education for
Tiara Club princesses, focusing on caring for animals
and the environment. The curriculum includes:

A visit to the Royal
County Show

Visits to the Country
Park and Bamboo Grove

Work experience on our
very own farm

Elephant rides in our
Safari Park (students
will be closely supervised)

Our headteacher, King Percy, is present at all times, and
students are well looked after by Fairy G, the school
Fairy Godmother.

Our resident staff and visiting experts include:

LADY WHITSTABLE KENT
(IN CHARGE OF THE FARM,
COUNTRY PARK AND SAFARI PARK)

QUEEN MOTHER MATILDA
(ETIQUETTE, POSTURE AND
APPEARANCE)

FAIRY ANGORA
(ASSISTANT FAIRY GODMOTHER)

FARMER KATE
(DOMESTIC ANIMALS)

LADY MAY (SUPERVISOR OF THE
HOLIDAY HOME FOR PETS)

We award tiara points to encourage our Tiara Club princesses towards the next level. All princesses who win enough points at Diamond Turrets will be presented with their Diamond Sashes and attend a celebration ball.

Diamond Sash Tiara Club princesses are invited to return to Golden Gates, our magnificent mansion residence for Perfect Princesses, where they may continue their education at a higher level.

PLEASE NOTE:
Princesses are expected to arrive at the Academy with a *minimum* of:

TWENTY BALLGOWNS
(with all necessary hoops, petticoats, etc)

TWELVE DAY DRESSES

SEVEN GOWNS
suitable for garden parties and other special day occasions

TWELVE TIARAS

DANCING SHOES
five pairs

VELVET SLIPPERS
three pairs

RIDING BOOTS
two pairs

Wellington boots, waterproof cloaks and other essential protective clothing as required

A farming we will go...and
I do SO hope you're going to come
with us! I'm Princess Bethany from
Tulip Room, and all my friends - that's
Caitlin, Lindsey, Abigail, Rebecca and
Mia - want me to say that they hope you
come with us, too! It's fun being here at
Diamond Turrets, but do you know what?
Sometimes I get a bit anxious about all
the animals here. PLEASE don't tell
anyone, but I secretly think cows
are a little bit scary...

Chapter One

I don't think any of us had ever seen our school fairy godmother, Fairy G, wearing rubber boots before – she looked so funny when she came stomping up the path to meet us for our very first farming lesson.

"Do you think she can fly in them?" Caitlin whispered in my ear.

I tried not to giggle. It's a little bit difficult to think of Fairy G flying, actually. She isn't exactly fairy-shaped – not like her assistant, Fairy Angora. Fairy Angora is very slim and pretty, but Fairy G is... I can't think of the right word without sounding rude. Comfortable, perhaps. But she's SO lovely, and she looks after us brilliantly.

"Now, princesses," she boomed. "You've got a wonderful morning ahead of you! Farmer Kate is going to take us to see the piglets, and after that she'll show you how to feed the adult pigs."

 and the Lost Piglet

The twins were standing near us, and I saw them look at each other and roll their eyes. "Yuck! Mummy would NEVER let us go near any horrible smelly pigs," Diamonde said loudly.

Fairy G frowned, and folded her arms. "You should know, Diamonde," she said crossly, "that pigs are extremely clean by nature. Farmer Kate's pigs live out in the orchards most of the time, and they most certainly do NOT smell! Now, please put your boots on, and we'll be off. Follow me, everyone!" And she set out towards the farm.

Diamonde made a face as she looked at the row of rubber boots lined up outside the back door. "If anyone thinks I'm going to wear such nasty clumpy things, they're wrong. 'A Perfect Princess should always look her very best', and I'M a Perfect Princess!" She stuck her nose in the air and walked on down the path, ignoring the boots completely.

"And I'm a Perfect Princess too!" Gruella echoed, as she followed Diamonde.

"You'll ruin your shoes," Rebecca called after them, but neither of them took the slightest notice.

We pulled on our boots, holding onto Lindsey's wheelchair to stop ourselves falling over. Mine were much too big for me; my mum had decided it would be sensible

to allow room for my feet to grow.
They slopped about as I walked,
and I hoped I'd never have to
run in them.

"Are...are pigs friendly?" I asked Mia, hoping my voice didn't sound wobbly.

"They're GORGEOUS!" she said, and her eyes shone. "My aunt had some on her estate, and they just loved it when I scratched their backs. Aunt Elisabetta says they're almost as intelligent as human beings! And piglets are the most glorious things in the whole wide world. I DO hope they let us hold one!"

That made me feel a little bit better, and my heart stopped fluttering. I know it was silly to be frightened of something I hadn't even seen, but I couldn't seem to help it. I think Abigail and Rebecca knew how I was feeling, because they smiled at me as Fairy G led us into one of the farm buildings.

When we saw the mother pig lying in the straw with her babies beside her, I completely forgot about being scared. She was AMAZING! She was really huge with big floppy ears, and I was surprised by how bristly she was. I'd always thought pigs were smooth and shiny. She was pink

with big black spots, but the piglets were much paler – almost white. They were spotty too – and they were absolutely BEAUTIFUL!

"There are so many of them!" I said in amazement, and I began to count. "...Eleven, twelve, thirteen, WOW! Just imagine having thirteen babies!"

Farmer Kate heard me, and she looked surprised. "Thirteen?" she asked. "Are you sure, Your Highness?" And she began to count as well. A moment later she nodded. "You're quite right. That means we've lost one. I do hope Gloria hasn't squashed it."

Chapter Two

We looked at Farmer Kate in horror. Surely she couldn't mean it? But she explained that sometimes mother pigs lie on their piglets by mistake.

"Gloria's a Gloucestershire Old Spot, and she's a marvellous mum – but as you can see, she IS very big. She wouldn't notice if she flumped down on top of one of her babies. We'll get her up and have a look – the piglets have had plenty of milk. They're eating solids now as well, so they won't be hungry."

I wasn't at all sure that I wanted

to see a squashed piglet, but it was OK. Kate whistled to Gloria, and pulled an apple out of her pocket. Gloria heaved herself up – and there was nothing underneath her but flattened straw.

We all sighed with relief...but then I thought, *So where's the piglet?*

Kate must have seen my face, because she said, "The littlest one is a bit of a daredevil." She pointed to the back of the sty, and we could see an opening rather like a super-sized cat flap leading to the field behind. "We're keeping Gloria in here for now, but the piglets can run in and out if they want to. They mostly stay inside; I'm hoping the littlest one has made up his mind to brave the big outdoors and is playing in the field somewhere. Maybe you'd like to have a look later, after you've fed the Whites and the Saddlebacks?"

"They're different kinds of pigs," Mia told us, when she saw us looking confused. Kate grinned at her. "Well done, Your Highness."

Behind us Diamonde sniffed loudly. "Fancy knowing all about pigs! I think we know what that says about Mia, Gruella!"

I didn't hear Gruella's answer, but I bet she agreed with her sister. Mia just ignored them; I do wish I could be like that.

"We'd love to look for the piglet," Rebecca told Kate, as Mia leant over to scratch Gloria's broad back.

"Right. That's settled." Kate looked pleased. "Now, Your Highnesses – if you go up to the top of the yard you'll see the back door to the school kitchens.

Hopefully the cooks will have put out a row of swill buckets. If you bring them back here, I'll show you what to do next."

"Swill buckets?" Gruella sounded completely horrified, and she turned to Fairy G. "Whatever are they? They sound REVOLTING!"

Fairy G gave her a chilly stare.

"It's a form of recycling, Gruella. Any leftover food from Diamond Turrets that's suitable for the pigs gets boiled up and put into buckets. Farmer Kate mixes in extra vitamins or anything else they need, and then it's poured into their troughs. You'll see for yourself how much they like it!"

Gruella went quite pale, and Diamonde clutched her forehead as if she were about to faint.

"YUCK..." she breathed. "Us feeding pigs? I DON'T think so..."

Fairy G began to swell up, which is never a good sign. It means she's getting angry.

"Diamonde! Gruella! You are here at the Royal Palace Academy for the Preparation of Perfect Princesses in order to LEARN! And thinking that you are too good to get your hands dirty is NOT the sign of a Perfect Princess. You will do exactly as Farmer Kate tells you, or I will report you to King Percy and Lady Whitstable-Kent, and there will be SERIOUS CONSEQUENCES!'

Diamonde and Gruella drooped, and Gruella whispered, "Sorry, Fairy G."

Fairy G huffed and puffed, and turned to the rest of us. "Perhaps

I should make it clear that ALL princesses are expected to do as they are asked WITHOUT complaining, arguing, or making a fuss. Is that understood?"

"Yes, Fairy G," we said as politely as we possibly could.

When Fairy G is angry she's scary; I couldn't imagine EVER arguing with her. She huffed a bit more, and then said she was returning to Diamond Turrets.

"I'll be coming back later with Lady Whitstable-Kent to see how you're getting on," she told us. "But for now I'll leave you with Farmer Kate!" And she stormed away in a cloud of fizzing stars.

Princess Bethany's stickers

The Tiara Club

Discover more magical stickers in the other Diamond Turrets books!

www.tiaraclub.co.uk

The Tiara Club series is written by Vivian French.

www.orchardbooks.co.uk

ORCHARD BOOKS

Chapter Three

I felt quite wobbly as Fairy G
disappeared into the distance.
I really hate it when she's cross with
us; even if I haven't done anything
wrong I still feel guilty. And I'm
scared stiff of Lady Whit (she's in
charge of the farm, the country
park and the safari park, while
King Percy is our headteacher).

Mia really likes her, but she makes me nervous, and when I'm nervous I drop things and look even sillier than usual.

We were all rather quiet as we walked up to the kitchens. Sure enough, there was a row of buckets waiting for us – and they were actually rather pretty. Each

bucket was painted with flowers, and Abigail looked much more cheerful as we got close enough to see them properly.

"Look!" she said. "Our buckets are painted with tulips, and they've got our names on them. Do you think that makes us REAL farmers?"

The stuff inside didn't look TOO dreadful; it was only boiled up peelings and bread and old cabbage leaves and things like that. We each found our own bucket and picked it up; they weren't very heavy, because they were only half full. The twins decided they'd carry Diamonde's bucket between them so they could hold their noses with their other hand.

"We're coming back for mine later," Gruella explained when she saw me looking at her.

"Poo!" Diamonde said, although I noticed she looked round first to make sure Fairy G wasn't anywhere

nearby. "This is SO disgusting!"

Farmer Kate was waiting for us, and she showed us how to mix in some chopped up apples and carrots. Then she pointed to a gate.

"If you go through there and down the track, you'll see the pig pens at the edge of the apple orchard. The troughs are behind a low wall, so you won't have to actually go in

with the pigs. Pour the swill in the troughs, making sure it's spread from one end to the other – and that's all there is to it. You can come back here and leave your buckets, and then go hunting for the missing piglet!"

"Thank you very much," we chorussed, and then we set off through the gate and down the track. Mia had to stop almost at once because she had a stone in her boot, and we waited while she fished it out – Tulip Room ALWAYS sticks together! It meant that we were behind everyone else, but we didn't mind.

Luckily it wasn't TOO muddy, and Lindsey was able to get along fine in her wheelchair, but I was very glad we had rubber boots on. There were loads of squelchy puddles.

"It's odd that Fairy G didn't notice Diamonde and Gruella still

had their shoes on, and not their boots," I said as Rebecca came to walk beside me.

Rebecca looked thoughtful. "Maybe she did notice, but she decided not to say anything. You never can tell what Fairy G is thinking."

"That's true!" Lindsey's eyes twinkled. "Perhaps she's hoping they'll get stuck in the mud, and that'll teach them a lesson."

"I can't see them anywhere," Caitlin said, "so they must be managing somehow."

It was fun swinging our buckets as we wandered along the track. It was the most gorgeous day, and we could hear birds singing, and sheep happily *baaing* in the fields further off.

"I do LOVE it here," Lindsey said as we reached the pig pens, and we all totally agreed with her.

When we peered over the low

wall we saw the troughs were already quite full, and masses of pigs were grunting and snuffling enthusiastically as they pushed and shoved their way to get at the food.

We tried not to empty our buckets on top of their heads, but it was difficult; several of them insisted on standing right in the troughs.

"There you are, boys and girls!" Caitlin said as she shook the last peelings out of her bucket. "Enjoy!"

Chapter Four

We looked round for the lost piglet as we made our way back, but we didn't see any sign of it. As we reached the yard I thought I saw something small and pink moving behind a large rose bush, but when I hurried round to look there wasn't any sign of a piglet – just the twins, who turned their backs on me and went on whispering to each other in their usual snooty kind of way.

"I must have imagined it," I told myself, and went to dump my bucket with the others. Then I went inside to join my friends, who were leaning over the rail while Kate showed them how to tickle Gloria behind her ears.

"Do come and try, Bethany! Mia said. "She just loves being scratched!"

"Shouldn't we go and look for the poor little piglet?" I asked. I couldn't help worrying about it, and wondering if it was scared all by itself in a big strange world.

"You're quite right." Abigail stood up. "Come on, everybody. Let's get going on a piglet hunt. Bethany – you lead the way!"

That made me smile. "Why don't we have a look in the yard outside first?" I suggested.

But Lady Whitstable suddenly appeared in the doorway. "Just one minute! You girls stay here! I want a word with Princess Bethany!"

She did NOT sound happy.

I hurried towards her, and she beckoned me outside and pointed to the buckets. "Would you please explain the meaning of this?"

I stood and stared, and my heart started doing cartwheels in my chest. There were our buckets, and they were all empty...except for mine! It was full to the brim; in fact, it looked much fuller than when I first picked it up.

"Fairy G told me there was a princess who thought she was too good to feed the pigs," Lady Whit snapped, "but I never thought it would be you, Bethany. This is NOT good enough. I'm MOST displeased. You're to go back to school right this minute, and explain your behaviour to King Percy." And she took my arm and began marching me along the path.

What would you have done? I'm sure Mia would have stood up for herself...but I couldn't think of anything to say. I almost wondered if I HADN'T fed the pigs. Lady Whit was making me walk so fast my brain felt as if it had been left behind, and all I could do was worry about what I was going to say to King Percy, and wonder how many minus tiara points I'd get. There was a huge lump in my throat, and I just KNEW that if our headteacher was cross I'd cry, even though I hadn't done anything wrong.

"Don't drag your feet!" Lady Whit said as we came to the school door. "Here at Diamond Turrets princesses have to learn to do as they're—"

She stopped, because the door burst open, and Fairy G stepped out in front of us so suddenly she and Lady Whit nearly bumped into each other.

"Goodness!" Fairy G said. "You ARE in a hurry!" And then she saw me, and she looked SO surprised. "Bethany? What are you doing here? Aren't you meant to be finding that little lost piglet?"

"I'm afraid Princess Bethany is in disgrace," Lady Whit said grimly. "It's just as you suspected. She did NOT go down to feed the pigs, and she's on her way to explain herself to King Percy!"

Chapter Five

Fairy G's eyebrows whizzed up her forehead. "But Lady Whit," she said, "are you quite sure? It wasn't Bethany I was talking about. It was..." she paused. "It was another princess. Or two."

"All the swill buckets were empty except for Bethany's," Lady Whit told her. "I saw it with my own eyes. It was full to the top..." Her voice died away, and a thoughtful expression floated over her face. "Actually, now I come to think about it, I asked the cooks to only half fill the buckets. How very odd!"

"I'd say we need to do a spot of detective work," Fairy G said cheerfully. "What do you think, Bethany?"

I swallowed hard. Was Fairy G going to save me? "Yes PLEASE!" I said. "Oh, PLEASE do!"

"Excellent! Come along, then." And Fairy G marched me and Lady Whit back down the path towards the farm buildings. "I think I'd like a look at our princesses. Bethany, you wait here while Lady Whit and I call them."

As Fairy G and Lady Whit strode off towards the orchard and the fields I sat down on a step to wait for them.

"Oink!"

It was such a tiny noise I thought at first I'd imagined it, but then I heard it again. "Oink!"

"Piggy?" I whispered, and the tiniest pig I'd ever seen peeped out from under the rose bush in the yard.

"Oh...piggy!" Hardly daring to breathe, I picked up an apple core from the full bucket, and held it out. "Here...piggy piggy!"

The piglet disappeared.

I stood up, and as quietly as I could I laid a trail of apple peelings. Once I'd finished, I hid in the doorway to watch...

and the Lost Piglet

and the piglet came out again.
"Oink!" it said, and it began to
gobble up the peelings. It came
nearer and nearer, and I grabbed
it, just as Farmer Kate came out of
the building, and Fairy G and
Lady Whit came stomping up

from the other direction. They were followed by the Diamond Turrets princesses.

"Well done, Your Highness!" Kate beamed at me, and took the piglet. "You deserve at least five tiara points!"

"Just a minute!" The twins suddenly popped out from behind the rose bush. "Actually, WE knew the piglet was hiding here," Diamonde announced. "Bethany would NEVER have caught it if we hadn't been watching to make sure it didn't go anywhere else. WE deserve tiara points as well!"

I stared at her in amazement. What did she mean? But Fairy G gave the twins a VERY stern look.

"Are you saying you've been behind that bush for some time, Diamonde?" she asked, and her voice was chilly.

Diamonde nodded. "Of course.

I told you. We were watching the piglet."

"I see." Fairy G began to grow, and I moved closer to Caitlin.

"And I also see something else. You are still wearing your ordinary shoes, and they're as clean as when you left the school this morning. I would suggest, Diamonde and Gruella, that you hid here instead of going to feed the pigs. That would be bad enough, but you are also guilty of a very nasty little deception. You emptied your buckets into Bethany's, and let her take the blame. Am I right?"

Diamonde began to protest, but Gruella said, "We didn't mean Bethany to be blamed. It was just that her bucket was nearest."

Lady Whit snorted loudly. "Well

I never! Princess Bethany, I'm so sorry. In future I'll be more careful before jumping to conclusions!"

"I think someone else owes Bethany an apology," Fairy G remarked, and there was a glint in her eye as she gave Diamonde a little push forward.

Diamonde hesitated, and then muttered, "Sorry, Bethany."

"I think you and your sister had better come with me," Lady Whit told her, and she turned to Fairy G. "I'm sure I can leave you to organise our picnic."

Fairy G shrank down to her normal size, and gave us all a wonderful smile. "Of course!"

Chapter Six

Do you like picnics? I LOVE them, and Fairy G's picnics are the best of all. She waves her wand, and tables heaped with delicious food come tumbling out of the air...and this was one of the very best ever! You wouldn't think a farm yard would be the ideal place, but Fairy G floated hanging wreaths of little pink roses over every building, and they looked utterly gorgeous. She even produced a magic harp, and the tunes tinkled SO sweetly as we chatted and laughed...and after we'd finished eating we could see

why she'd chosen to stay in the yard. The harp played lots of bouncy hoppitty tunes, and we danced and danced round the yard in our muddy boots. Fairy G said we still looked like the most Perfect Princesses!

And guess what? Just as we were getting tired, Kate came out carrying the tiny piglet, and we all took turns in holding him – and when it was my turn he said

OINK! especially loudly, then closed his eyes and went to sleep on my lap. Kate said he must have recognised me, and decided I was a nice person. I was SO proud.

*

And that night as we got ready for bed I realised I was proud of something else as well. I was REALLY proud that I had six very special friends who kept me company, even if things went wrong.

Five friends in Tulip Room – and you!

Don't miss **The Tiara Club** website at:

www.tiaraclub.co.uk

Keep up to date with the latest
Tiara Club books and meet all
your favourite princesses!

There is SO much to see and do,
including games and activities. You can
even become an exclusive member of the
Tiara Club Princess Academy.

PLUS, there are exciting
competitions with truly
FABULOUS prizes!

Be a Perfect Princess – check it out today!

What happens next?
Find out in

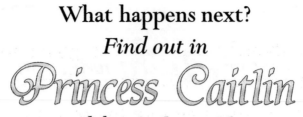

and the Little Lamb

Hello! How are you doing?
I'm Princess Caitlin, and I'm
very, VERY pleased to meet you!
Have you met the rest of Tulip Room
here at Diamond Turrets? There's
Amelia, and Bethany, Lindsey, Abigail and
Rebecca – and me and you, of course.
It's wonderful here, even though
the twins, Diamonde and Gruella,
are always causing trouble...

I thought Lindsey was going to burst with excitement when she came zooming into the recreation room. It was just before bedtime, and she'd been to look at the school notice board to see if we had an extra art lesson the next day. Mia thought we did, but I was sure we didn't.

Anyway, Lindsey came whizzing back, her cheeks bright pink and her eyes sparkling. She very nearly ran Diamonde over, and of course Diamonde screeched – but for once Lindsey didn't stop to apologise.

"LOOK!" she said, and she waved a piece of paper under our

noses. "It's a competition, and the winner gets to lead a little orphan lamb in the Grand Procession at the Royal County Show!"

We all practically smothered Lindsey as we tried to see the paper at once, and she burst out laughing.

"I'll read it to you," she said. "'All princesses are invited to create a costume suitable for farm work. You may work individually, in pairs, or in a group of not more than six. Consideration must be given to comfort and practicality before elegance. Princesses will be expected to wear their costumes on the day of the Royal County Show. There will be a formal parade at ten o'clock, and the entries will be judged by her most Gracious Majesty Queen Frizella Marie—'"

"WHAT'S THAT?" Diamonde absolutely GRABBED the paper out of Lindsey's hand.

"Just wait a minute!" I said indignantly, staring at Diamonde. "Lindsey was reading that!"

Diamonde gave me a snooty stare back. "Actually, Caitlin, Queen Frizella Marie is our great aunt, so we know who'll win, don't we, Gruella?"

Gruella looked very surprised. "Do we?"

Diamonde gave a heavy sigh. "US, of course!"

"But Queen Frizella Marie isn't the only judge," Lindsey pointed out. "There are three names on the list."

Diamonde frowned, and looked at the paper again. "Lady Whitstable-Kent, King Percy and Queen Frizella Marie. The school farm manager, our headteacher, and the most important queen for miles and miles and MILES around. H'm. Well, we know who's the most important of those three, don't we, Gruella?"

"Oh yes," Gruella simpered. "King Percy. He's SO handsome."

Diamonde went bright purple. "Honestly, Gruella," she snapped, "sometimes you don't see what's under your nose. WE are going to win, because Queen Frizella Marie is sure to choose us. Come on! Let's go and design our winning costume!" And she seized her twin's arm, bundling her out of the recreation room.

"Goodness," Rebecca said as the door slammed shut behind them. "Do you think she's right?"

Mia laughed. "No," she said.

"King Percy would never have asked anyone to judge the competition who wasn't going to be fair."

~∽ *Want to read more?* ∽~
Princess Caitlin and the Little Lamb
is out now!